How the
REINDEER
Got Their Antlers

For Catriona
G. McC.

For Bea
H. H.

Text copyright © 2000 by Geraldine McCaughrean
Illustrations copyright © 2000 by Heather Holland
All Rights Reserved
Printed in Hong Kong
First published in Great Britain in 2000 by Orchard Books
First published in the United States by Holiday House in 2000
FIRST EDITION

Library of Congress Cataloging-in-Publication Data
McCaughrean, Geraldine.
How the reindeer got their antlers / by Geraldine McCaughrean ;
illustrated by Heather Holland.—1st ed.
p. cm.
Summary: Ashamed of her crown of antlers, the reindeer retreats
to the lonely northern wastelands, but many years later her descendants
find their antlers useful when they help Santa Claus one Christmas Eve.
ISBN 0-8234-1562-7 (hardcover)
[1. Reindeer—Fiction. 2. Antlers—Fiction.
3. Christmas—Fiction. 4. Santa Claus—Fiction. 5. Individuality—Fiction.]
I. Holland, Heather, ill. II. Title.
PZ7.M1286 Ho 2000
[E]-dc21   99-049961

How the REINDEER Got Their Antlers

by Geraldine McCaughrean
illustrated by Heather Holland

Holiday House / New York

As soon as the animals were made,
they began to quarrel about who should be King.
  "I am the fiercest," said Lion.
  "I am the noisiest," said Rooster.
  "I am the smartest," said Penguin.
  "But I am the best," said proud little Reindeer.

An angel held up his hands. "When the Maker made you, he did not make you in order of greatness. To show that he thinks of you all as kings and queens, I shall give you all crowns."

So, on each head he placed a different crown: a wreath of fur for Lion, a scarlet coxcomb for Rooster, a black-and-white crest for Penguin, and something special for Reindeer.

No sooner were the crowns given out than
the animals began to quarrel about whose
crown was best.

"Mine is biggest!"

"Mine is brightest!"

"Mine is prettiest!"

"But mine is . . . horrible!" cried proud little Reindeer.
Staring at her reflection, she saw that the angel
had given her a crown like a lopped tree.

To stop the animals from quarreling, the angel
gave them kingdoms in different parts of the world.

The lions he sent to the grassy plains,

the roosters
to the farmyards,

the penguins to the
gleaming South.

But turning to little
Reindeer, he found her gone.
Ashamed of her ugly, knobby crown, she had run away,
away from the stares and laughter of the other animals,
away from the glaring sunlight.

As she ran, she passed through deserts.
How good it would be to feel hot sand
underfoot each day, she thought, but dared not
stop in the desert.

She passed through fields of crops. How good
it would be to nibble on green plants every day,
she thought, but dared not stop in the fields.

She passed through woodlands. How good
it would be to stand in the dappled shade, she
thought, but dared not stop for fear of being seen.

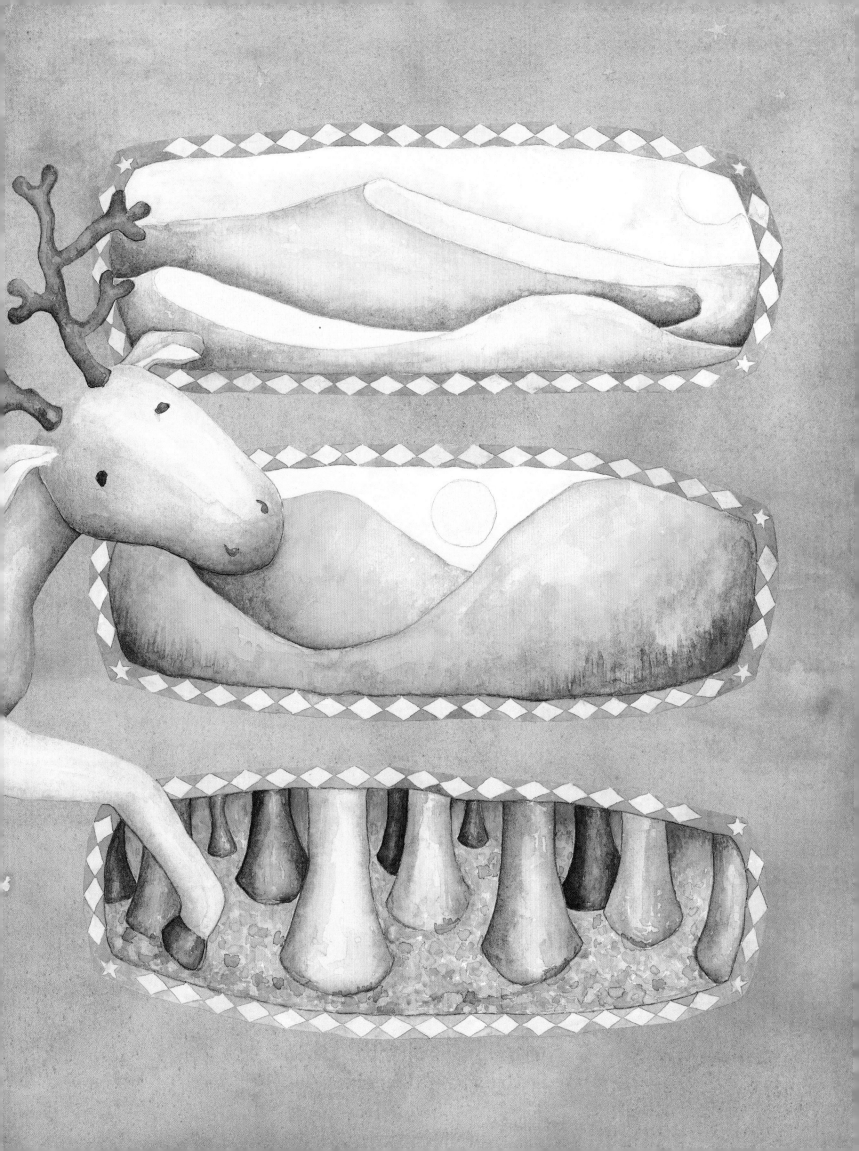

On and on she ran, to the farthest,
coldest regions of the earth, where no other
animals cared to live. And there she made a home.
Her children, and her children's grandchildren, were
born amid the snow and ice: a thousand generations,
and each with a crown of antlers. For ten thousand
years, the reindeer hid themselves away.

Then, one winter day, a man in a coat of
red was pulling his sleigh across a frozen lake.

But he slipped—bump!—and fell on his bottom.

"Every year my load gets bigger. I'll have
to find someone to help me pull my sleigh."
He tried to get to his feet, but the ice was
glassy smooth.

Bump! He sat down again.

So Santa Claus cupped his mittened hands to his mouth and bellowed with all his might. His shout carried all over the world.

"Who will help me pull my sleigh? I must deliver my cargo tonight!"

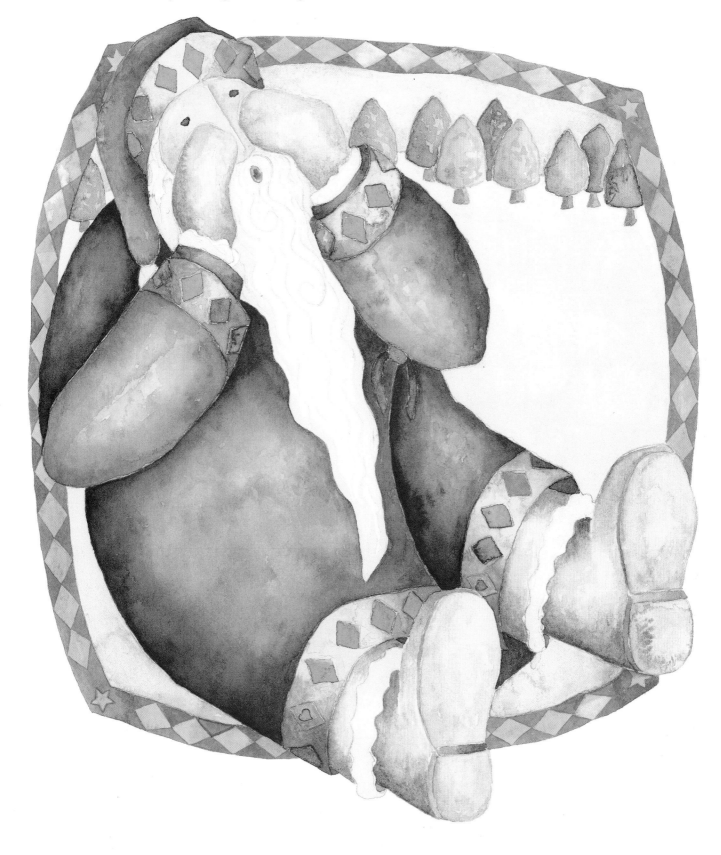

"Not I," said Lion. "I've done enough today."

"Not I," said Rooster. "That sleigh is too heavy for me."

"Not I," said Penguin. "I see enough of ice and snow."

The reindeer peeped out from behind the
frosted trees and said, "We will pull your sleigh
for you . . . if we are not too ugly."

"My dear friends!" said Santa. "You are a
very welcome sight!"

The soft-frogged feet of the reindeer did not
slip on the ice, and when Santa had climbed in
among the bright packages, they set off across
the frozen lake.

"What is in your parcels that must be delivered tonight?" asked the littlest reindeer.

"Why, Christmas presents, of course!" said Santa. But the reindeer had never heard of Christmas.

"Once a year I deliver presents to every good girl and boy," he explained as the reindeer trotted over the ice, "but it must be done on Christmas Eve. No other night will do. Tell me, friends, why do you live in such a lonely place as this?"

"We hide ourselves away because of our ugly crowns," they replied.

"Then tomorrow, to thank you for your help, I shall give you all golden crowns in place of your antlers. That shall be your Christmas present!"

At that very moment, the silver blades of the sleigh slid over thin ice. With a lurch, the sleigh began to slide backward into the water!

"The tree! Reach for the tree!" cried the littlest reindeer.
With that, the oldest reindeer stretched out her neck and
wedged her antlers in the branches of a fir tree.

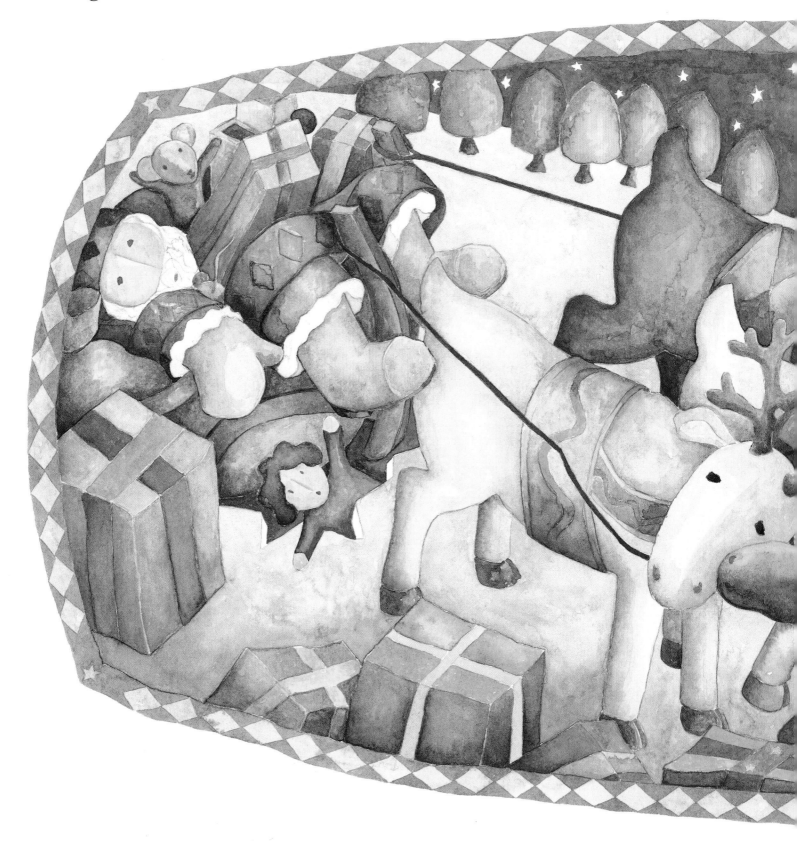

The others tangled their horns in the harness straps.
Then they p-u-l-l-e-d. And no one pulled harder than
the littlest reindeer.

They heaved and strained and they hauled the sleigh . . .

. . . to safety.

When it was done, they looked a sorry sight, their antlers broken, the ice strewn with velvet.

"You dear, wonderful, marvelous . . . !" exclaimed Santa, mopping his face. "Now you really will need those golden crowns!"

But the oldest reindeer said, "I think not, thank you. Gold is soft and bends too easily. Gold would have been no use tonight."

Another nodded. "Over the years, our necks and heads have grown big and muscular. Pretty crowns might make us look foolish . . . "

". . . or even uglier," said a third.

"And we may be ugly, but we are very brave!" declared the littlest reindeer, holding his head high.

"Ugly? Bless me!" said Santa. "You're the best, most handsome animals in the world! I'll just have to think of another present, that's all."

Ever since that night, the reindeer
have helped Santa Claus deliver his
presents on Christmas Eve. Now, though, they draw
the Christmas sleigh not over snowdrifts and frozen lakes,
but out across the night sky among the tinsel stars.

For his present to them was the yearly gift of flight
one single, magical night of soaring over desert,
woods, and fields.

Despite the sights they see spread out below,
they are now so fond of their lonely northern
lands where the moon fills the sky and the
Northern Lights pour down that they no longer
wish to live anywhere else.

Every year, though the youngest reindeer look eagerly among their presents for a crown, it is a crown of antlers they are hoping to find.

For as you and I and the full moon know, antlers are the pride of any reindeer.